BEST

SEAT

IN THE

HOUSE

Best Seat in the House

Michelle Young

Rock Forest Publishing

Cover Design by Michelle Young

ISBN-13: 978-1-7388012-6-8
Best Seat In The House / Michelle Young
Rock Forest Publishing

ALSO BY MICHELLE YOUNG

Salt & Light
Without Fear
Your Move
There She Lies
The Sleep Clinic
Cages
Bookish Notebook
One More Chapter
Mama Elephant's Baby Tiger
See You Sunday

DEDICATION

To all the odd, passed-down, used, eclectic, and accent pieces—may you find those who will cherish you.

CHAPTER 1

I remember the day my owners found me. I'd been sitting at the end of the driveway with the afternoon sun fighting against oppressing clouds. My owners' truck bed had been brimming with so many items that there had hardly been any room left for me.

Nevertheless, something about me had caught their eye. They'd made room in their truck and, coincidently, in their hearts, giving me a new chance, a new life, and more joy than I ever knew was possible.

My old owner, George, hadn't taken me to his new room at the retirement home. We'd been together for close to 40 years. I was practically a part of the family by then.

But none of George's kids had the same affinity for me as their father had. They'd discarded me the very weekend George moved out. His new room was too small to accommodate a bed, dresser, and me. I know it must have been hard for him to part ways with me, but such is life.

It's rare for someone like me to only have one owner. So, for that and all the memories George gave me over our time together, I'm forever grateful. He'd been a hell of an owner, and I will forever cherish the memories we shared. I can't say the same of his children, however.

Those brats never knew a good thing if it was staring them in the face. Kids these days. All about leather, shiny metal, gray everything, and plain boring design styles. What was this new obsession with *modernizing* lately? There was just no more room for a classic style like me anymore, it seemed.

I'd seen it time and time again from my place near the window. One piece after another would eventually end up at the road, sometimes with a paper tapped to it announcing its apparently worthless value, the blocky four letters written crudely in a sharpie marker on a ripped piece of paper, flapping in the breeze. 'Free', as though owning such a rare item was burdensome and would someone, anyone, please take it off their hands as quickly as possible?

Early on garbage collection morning, unfortunate pieces would sometimes miss the opportunity to be spotted by a new owner before someone picked them up and tossed them in the back of a garbage truck, crushing them to pieces in one fell swoop.

2

It had been horrible to watch these timely, gorgeously custom-built pieces—most of them hand-carved, and expertly upholstered—get obliterated in a matter of seconds. You just didn't see that kind of craftsmanship anymore.

Furniture nowadays barely lasts the year. It's all about production. With flimsy frames, particle board contraptions, most of them built swiftly on an assembly line, without any love or care whatsoever, not to mention the prominent reduction of stuffing in the cushions. I'm not sure what manufacturers used these days, but that cheap stuff barely lasts the year. The perfect way to ruin a back, I'd say!

I come from a time when people simply built things differently. Sure, there weren't as many of us the year I came around, but that's how it used to be. People used to know how to wait for things. They used to appreciate good things when they saw them. Now, they dump everything they no longer wish to keep in a truck and place it in a field on top of another pile of discarded mess, pretending to 'redecorate' or claiming that the piece suddenly became uncomfortable. So much waste.

Luckily, George had never treated me as something he could simply abandon. He'd valued and cared for me as I had for him. So it had been quite a shock when his kids put me at the curb that day. I felt outraged on behalf of George. If he'd only known how his kids had treated me, his one prized possession. He wouldn't have stood for it. But alas, George hadn't had a say in the matter. He wasn't one to argue with reason. There just hadn't been sufficient space for all his favorite pieces in his tiny room at the retirement home. They had made sacrifices.

Perhaps I should have expected his children to want to get rid of me so eagerly. And yet, part of me had held onto a sliver of hope that there would be enough sentimentality left of me to not get thrown out with the garbage. Thankfully for me, George's kids had had the decency to give me one last chance to find a new home and had organized a garage sale. However, from the meek turn-out, it appeared that they hadn't advertised the sale well or offered the proper directions. They seemed to be solely relying on people driving by on their own accord, not really caring if anything sold, seeing this as yet another task in their already busy schedules.

The odds seemed to be against me. Between my outdated style, age, and my odd coloring, I wasn't the stunner I'd once been. Most people didn't know what to make of my odd fabric color. It had often been the source of many conflicting opinions as it was never properly determined as either green or blue.

Everyone seemed to be chasing after various shades of grey these days and I most definitely did not fit that category, no matter what light shined over me or how much you squinted. I've always considered myself to be in the teal family, but whatever it was, my pigment seemed to do little else than deter people from choosing me time and time again. My bright, uncertain color distressed or confused people more often than not, leaving their design plans befuddled and finding myself abandoned once more.

All this to say that on that fall afternoon, I'd all but given up hope and begrudgingly begun to accept my fate of being left out overnight, knowing full-well by the thick clouds hanging low in the sky, that I'd get pelted by rain before most people got home for dinner.

It was at that precise moment when the black truck came around the bend. I shrunk and my legs dug into the gravel driveway. I was feeling sorry for myself, when movement caught my eye. The truck, curving sleekly from the other end of the street like a skilled water snake, cruising lazily, inched closer towards us.

Hope had swelled within me, filling the concave parts of me, making me straighten up. It was mid-afternoon by then. The sun had been hiding behind the threatening clouds, and it was quickly cooling down. Terrified of the very likely chance that the truck would simply drive right past the driveway, I'd stubbornly swallowed my pride and forced myself to stand tall. This was my last chance, and I'd known it. I'd had to make the most of it.

The truck had slowed to a crawl and then finally, it had pulled over to the shoulder, stopping right next to the driveway's entrance. The woman got out first, jumping down from the passenger side, her black sneakers landing swiftly on the plush grass, a wide grin on her face as she'd eyed me from across the lawn. With a giddy, childlike excitement, she approached me, trying and failing to hide her enthusiasm at having finally found the missing piece in her collection.

The man, her husband, I'd presumed by the way he'd walked around the front of the truck and held out a hand for her to grasp, had strode towards me with a purposeful assurance that had made me instantly calmer. There had been no doubt about their interest, no second-guessing, no hemming and hawing about how I would fit into their lives.

The way they'd regarded me had instantly reassured me. I'd be saved after all, despite all the odds. Someone still saw worth in me. These strangers had given me confidence that there was still enough left of me for someone to love. Even George's kids, whom I'd watched grow up and held between my armrests on holidays, hadn't offered me the same level of decency.

Standing before me, wide grins on their faces, I'd known that whatever they had in mind for me, I wanted to be at the center of it. Their interest clearly demonstrated that they would make space for me, work around me, display me, and love me like George had when he'd first spotted me through that storefront display window.

I didn't know what the likelihood of me landing two sets of incredible owners in my lifetime was, but I considered myself very lucky indeed.

From the looks of it, the couple had been busy gathering a variety of pieces that hardly seemed to fit together. Somehow, I'd just understood. The items would work perfectly for that very same reason.

I knew what I had to offer and made no illusions about my age. My wear and tear were obvious the moment they'd laid eyes on me. Even so, my imperfections hadn't seemed to deter them. The price tag taped to me had fluttered in the rising breeze. It had almost been like a white flag, beckoning them to pay attention to the predicament I would find myself in if they did not load me onto their truck at that exact moment.

They hadn't even bothered trying me out before offering to pay the sale price.

Seeing the value and not bothering with negotiations, the couple had happily paid much less than I knew I was worth, but much more than most would have for a pre-owned, pre-loved piece such as myself.

Their interest and the genuine smiles on their faces were reason enough for me, but it hadn't hurt to be treated with respect. It might have baffled some to know what they paid to own me. But they'd seen beyond the age and out-of-style aspects. In fact, I think they'd found it endearing, a selling factor.

I could hardly believe my luck when they'd hoisted me on top of the enormous pile of furniture and strapped me in next to an elegant Queen Anne high back—a stunning piece I'd hoped to get the chance to spend more time with. Things were already starting to look up. They'd secured me with rope just as tiny droplets of rain started coming down. I could feel my muscles relax as they drove away from the only home I'd ever known and onto my next adventure.

At that moment, George crossed my mind and I dared to believe he would have been happy to see me off on a new beginning. I know that his leaving me behind hadn't been an easy decision for him. I sincerely think that he'd assumed his children would have graciously welcomed an old classic like me into their homes. Unfortunately, George had been sadly mistaken. So blinded by his love and appreciation for me that he'd failed to notice the disdain in his children's eyes every time I'd come up in conversation.

It doesn't matter now. Everything happens for a reason. George had been a wonderful first owner, and I will be forever grateful for the kindness and attention he's given me over the years.

But that's now in the past. I was looking ahead, embarking on a new journey, heading towards my new home.

The couple unloaded me from the bed of the truck first as though the most precious of all their found treasures that day. In reality, they'd had no choice but to remove me first, seeing as I'd been the last one strapped in.

Moving every piece inside, carefully avoiding the sharp edges of the front doorframe, they'd lifted me together, removed their shoes on the entrance rug, and glided me across the house from room to room, trying to find an ideal spot to place me.

After quite a bit of deliberation, I'd finally found a home beside a bay window at the front of the house. I would later learn that this was the front living room.

Their steps echoed across the empty room. They'd placed me down gently on the carpeted floor. My new owners moved in the rest of their newly acquired furniture swiftly and with the efficiency of people who'd worked together for years. They were careful, considering the entire space before adding new items.

The finishing touch and most delightful surprise was in my closest companion. They placed the cream colored, slender Queen Anne beside me for many years to come. I'd be lying if I said I wasn't giddy at the prospect that we might someday become much more than neighbors.

But for now, I contended with her proximity to me and the fact that she, along with this large window, would be my view for the foreseeable future.

In this home, they didn't criticize me for my odd coloring, but rather, they praised it.

They'd called me, `The accent chair'. I'd worn that name with the utmost pride. The woman spent weeks, if not months, deliberating every design element of the space and eventually used my very pigment to add pops of color throughout the house.

To say I felt flattered would be an understatement. I experienced utter delight to be cherished in this manner. It soon became evident to me that the couple were just as grateful for me as I was for them.

My post by the window offered me much entertainment, as well as glimpses of information into my new owners' lives. From my perch, I'd been able to observe their progress of working in the yard. They'd been relentless; pruning old perennials, trimming the overgrown lilac bushes, cutting down dead trees, digging up peonies, and transplanting plants to other sections of the garden, taking great care not to damage the delicate roots. They worked tirelessly, so focused and determined to turn this house into a home they would be proud of.

I'd adored being by the window and would occupy this very spot for years, standing vigil like a loyal soldier until they found it necessary to move me some place new.

In this first location, however, I had many fond memories of a delicious wood-burning fireplace warming me in the cooling evenings and of a knitted throw laid over one of my armrests.

At first, I assumed that the man would choose me as his favorite seating choice, considering how tall and broad-shouldered he was compared to the woman. He had similar mannerisms to George, too, which drew me to him automatically. It was like a reborn inner need for his attention, and I craved it. A man of his stature deserved comfort and support, which I was more than happy to offer. After all, that was the purpose for which I had been created.

But, to my astonishment, although perhaps this should have been obvious to me, the woman claimed me as her own. It seemed obvious in retrospect that she would be the one to choose me.

She'd been the one urging the truck to halt in order to collect me in the first place, so it should have come to no surprise. This left the man to select the Queen Anne for himself.

I'd cringed and worried if her slender legs could support his weight, but she'd held her own, impressively sturdy for what most people would use as decorative seating. She seemed to welcome the challenge. I'd quickly learned just how stubborn she could be. Either she'd been trying to impress me or attempting to prove to herself that she still had it. Either way, I was more in awe of her with every passing day.

The woman would often sit on me, her legs curled beneath the throw, clutching a large glass of red wine in her hand while the other held onto a book. Merlot, the couple's cat, would jump on the woman's lap and snuggle in the crook of her arm, reading and relaxing under the soft light of the new standing lamp my owners had placed just behind me.

For hours, I held her like that, enjoying the twisted thrillers she seemed so fond of, often scaring myself with the plot twists, amazed at how exciting words on a page could be.

George had never been much of a reader, preferring television shows instead. His favorites had been Law & Order, Seinfeld, and the odd John Wayne movie.

Where George had smelled of old cheddar cheese, *Head and Shoulders* shampoo, and car grease from his work as a mechanic, the woman smelled of vanilla, spicy wine, and dusty old books. She never seemed to mind the upholstered buttons digging into her back or the way the seat cushion sometimes slid away and had to be repositioned. I was glad to have retained a comfortable stuffing ratio for she spent so many hours in my company. Otherwise, I'd have worried about her back muscles growing sore had she chosen a more modern seat. She never complained when she sat on me, if anything, she seemed to claim that my high back was good for her posture.

Some of my most cherished memories of those early years, are when she'd been reading beneath the lamp, her empty wine glass long since discarded on the coffee table, and the pages of her book turning slower as her head began to lean more heavily on my wings. I'd often gotten the honor of cradling her as she'd read herself to sleep.

I was no fancy Chesterfield High-Back chair, but I could still get the job done. It was my pride and joy to offer such comfort to my owners.

CHAPTER 2

I soon became a favorite seating choice to my owners but also to everyone who visited them. They seemed to have an open-door policy, always welcoming anyone who would grace their front door. I'd heard of their financial trouble, but at their smiling, grateful faces, and carefully prepared meals, you'd never guess it.

There always seemed to be enough food for whoever stopped by unannounced. Something always seemed to be baking in the oven and would fill their home with aromas of sweetness and spices. The fireplace was nearly always lit in the colder seasons, which suited me just fine. In my old age, I welcomed such comforts and thought it very considerate of them.

As social as they seemed to be, the couple also appreciated the quiet times they got to spend together. Sharing a pot of English Breakfast tea or sitting on the floor around the large (second-hand) wooden coffee table, picking from an assortment of cured meats, soft cheeses, sliced baguette, red grapes, and salty nuts, chewing and conversing quietly, as though subdued by the flicker of the flame dancing in the fireplace. They often celebrated weekends by uncorking a bottle of red wine, sipping from large, stemmed glasses, while engaging in lively hours-long political, social, or spiritual debates. Often, they'd still be talking well after the fire went out.

I had enjoyed listening to them discuss what mattered to them, being a silent observer of their comings and goings. I'd considered myself extremely lucky to be at the center of all their important discussions, hearing points being made on both sides, rejoicing with them, but also feeling torn when arguments occurred. Thankfully, they didn't seem to disagree on things that often. The respect and love they had for each other was quite beautiful to witness. I felt honored to be such a central part of their lives as they spent so much time in my company.

For some reason, they'd often chosen to sit together on the carpeted floor rather than on me. Instead, they'd lean their backs against me as though I was a mere resting post. They'd appeared to prefer each other's closeness to my comfortable cushions. Whenever they'd rested against me like this, I'd found it rather difficult to stay still as the man's short and fluffy hair would tickle me every time he moved his head.

Once upon a time, I'd come as part of a set, completed by a footrest ottoman. Unfortunately, we got separated many years ago after George's dog, Rosco, a Labrador Retriever, bit into it so severely that it became irreparable.

Rosco had gone off to training school that very week, so thankfully, I'd been spared the same fate. Unlike my unfortunate partner, I'd had the luxury of spending my days with a well-mannered pup. Still, I'd never quite forgiven Roscoe for separating me from my better half. I'd also never truly let my guard down in his company.

The dog was around for many years, bringing George an unexpected and undervalued amount of joy. To his kids, Rosco was a nuisance they couldn't wait to get rid of. The grandkids had other opinions, however, and rejoiced in the dog's presence, often running to him the moment they entered the house and never leaving his side until it was time for them to return home.

Rosco had loved the attention, and I'd enjoyed the break his distraction afforded me. The kids would throw toys from a nearby basket, taking turns tugging on bone-shaped cloths, trying and failing to tire the pup who never seemed to run out of energy.

George was always so happy to have his family together, watching the action from his seat, clapping a hand over his knee whenever Rosco would dodge one of the children's attempts to grab his toy from him.

George's wife had left years before. Good riddance, if you asked me. She'd been a nasty woman, always picking on him, telling him to pick up his shoes or do some odd jobs around the house the very moment George would settle down. She never let him rest.

It was like she was jealous of the amount of time George and I spent together. She was always trying to get him moving up and out of his seat. So many times, I'd wanted to yell at her to just let the poor man relax for a moment or two, but she never seemed to notice all the hours he'd spent on his feet.

George's job had been exhausting and demanding. He'd always be lifting heavy parts, crouching in odd positions, stretching his muscles or causing his back chronic pain. She hadn't spent intimate time studying his posture or his sore muscles the way I'd had. No one had known him as well as I had. With me, George would let his guard down. That was the best compliment I could ever have received.

Whenever we'd be together, George was free to just be himself. He didn't have to worry about how stiff he was or how long he'd used me for. There had been no one to impress or shame him whenever he laughed at a silly joke on television.

When George's wife left him, he'd been a little melancholic for a few weeks, lost in thought, his body sagging more than usual. He'd spent many hours in the dark in complete silence, but I'd just sat there with him, waiting patiently for this phase to pass. Soon, as I'd predicted, he'd finally regained his fervor, finding joy in the old things he'd used to do.

He'd been able to see how toxic his marriage had been and how much better off he was on his own.

George and his wife often felt too exhausted to repeat conversations, which filled the house with heavy silence. However, when she left, the house was emptier without her but fuller with the sounds of laughter that resonate against the walls every evening as George and I settled together before the television.

In my new house, however, my owners never appeared to watch much television. In fact, the room they'd placed me in upon my arrival had no television at all. The odd night, I'd heard laughter coming from a screen as the woman watched *Friends* on repeat while her husband worked late. But from my spot, I hadn't managed to glimpse the screen no matter how much I'd stretched. Instead, I'd found pleasure in simply listening, pretending the show was playing on the radio instead, laughing along with Chandler's sarcastic comments and Ross' whiny voice.

It had been difficult for me to be so far away from the woman during these times because I'd learned after a few months of living here, that she only seemed to retreat to that room and watch that show as a way to comfort herself whenever she'd been feeling sad.

It was something she'd started doing more and more, leaving me to collect a thin film of dust on my cushions. The happy seasons came and went, and she'd find me again, waiting for her in the front living room, a reassuring and constant presence she could always rely on. She'd fluff my cushions and pat the dust away, sometimes resolving to use a lint roller to lift Merlot's cat hair from the seat before settling down in it.

Books brought her a different kind of comfort; I'd soon figured out. They were a way for her to escape reality.

Whereas television shows offered a background noise to her intrusive thoughts, allowing her to stare at passing images without having to concentrate much on them.

There definitely seemed to be a regular pattern to her preference to choose television or books. She would seesaw between them like a revolving door, until she'd eventually succumbed to her darkness and became physically ill. Leaving the home would cause her to fall to shambles, only to swiftly be replaced with a surprising surge of energy and happiness that brightened the entire mood of the space.

I learned to anticipate the rise and fall of her moods, knowing when I'd be needed and when she'd found solace elsewhere. I could have been petty about it, wanting to have her all to myself, but I'd decided early on to be there for her whenever she'd need me.

She always came back to me eventually, never choosing the Queen Anne over me, unless, of course, a visitor otherwise occupied me.

I seemed to be her first choice of seating. It had made me feel incredibly precious and rare, although I was anything but. There were others like me. I just hadn't met many of them in my time.

The day I was made over 40 years ago, was a blur of sawdust, a loud and jarring hand saw, the pulse of a terrifying nail gun that I'd prefer never to encounter again, and the stench of a strong glue that burned my eyes.

The manufacturing plant had been on the smaller side, but they would produce the most beautiful pieces, renowned and sought out by many.

Pieces were often on back order or custom-made for a specific customer. The small square footage of the shop held only a handful of woodworkers, only one of which was skilled in upholstery.

There was never a dull moment in that shop, with the radio blasting and the guys sharing pleasantries, laughing along to inside jokes. They'd taken great care of the pieces they'd produced. Quality and comfort seemed to be values they'd uphold with the most importance. I'd inherited the same values from my time spent amongst them.

I'd seen many gorgeous and unique pieces being carefully assembled during my stay at the store. It never ceased to amaze me; all the work and attention to detail involved in the creation of pieces like me.

The young lad tasked to build me had started off by taking great care with my frame. Using the most beautiful slab of oak wood, with distinct knots carefully displayed, he'd proudly worked over me for weeks. Starting with shaping my arms, he'd painstakingly made a slight curve at the wrists, giving me an elegance I didn't feel I deserved.

The strong glue had burned his eyes, but he'd been mindful of his application, careful not to dab too much for it might spill off the sides and risk ruining the final look. The robust frame was a piece of art. He'd spent hours perfecting every angle, adding dowels, glue, and clamps whenever necessary. He'd built me so solidly, ensuring I would last for decades. I'm proud to be a living testimony of his hard work. I felt like the sturdiest chair in the whole workshop.

He'd put so much effort into making me look my best, and I was so grateful for it.

There'd been a lot of pressure on the young man to build the best piece he possibly could. His budding talent had to be proven to the staff, and I was lucky enough to be the recipient.

He'd spent a long while meticulously tending to me, until the day he'd come into the shop appearing haggard and messy. He'd had puffy, dark circles beneath his eyes, but more prominently, he'd been sporting a black eye.

When the shop keeper had questioned him about it, the lad had initially been reluctant to offer an explanation. Once alone with the shop keeper, I'd heard him admit that his old man had gotten rough with him. The lad's father regularly had a temper. It had made me sad to see the young man flinch in pain whenever he forgot himself and rubbed sawdust from his eyes as he opened up emotional wounds.

They didn't wear protective glasses back then, nor did they use masks. It wouldn't surprise me if that boy developed lung issues due to the inhalation of all the tiny dust particles floating around him as the workers built piece after piece. I haven't thought of him in ages. He must be well into his sixties now. I wonder if ever got married or had any kids? Has he been able to build a better relationship with his father? For someone who'd spent such a long time making sure every piece he worked on was perfectly and solidly built, I never got the chance to get to know him as intimately as he'd known me.

The day he came in with the black eye, he'd been unusually and understandably antsy and very distracted.

He'd tripped over buckets of screws, put things in the wrong places, and had gotten upset with himself more than on any other day. He'd been so hard on himself; it had been difficult to watch. I'd wished I'd been able to talk to him; shown him the wonderful care and attention he'd had for me.

His father might not have seen any value in him, but I'd certainly had. In hindsight, it's not unexpected that on this day, as he was securing my legs to the frame, he made errors, took shortcuts, and ultimately made a mess. I don't think he'd intentionally glazed over certain steps or meant to skip important details, but his mistakes had ended up costing my new owners a lot of grief and a bunch of money.

There were only two other chairs being built at the same time as me, each of us at different stages of completion. The building stage was the shortest of a chair's life, so I only remained in the sawdust globe for a few months. Then, they moved me to a different section of the shop and covered me up.

The Upholsterer was a man in his fifties, a Frenchman named Hugo that seemed to be respected by all, not necessarily for his eccentric personality, but for his craftsmanship. He wore a thick, black Fu Manchu style mustache with long ends that curved down against his chin, carefully styled this way with an obscene amount of gel.

It looked purposefully obnoxious and pompous, but it suited him perfectly. He wore his thinly rimmed, gold glasses propped up on the tip of his nose, enhancing his comically original style. It's a wonder how those tiny metal wires could hold up the thick lenses he required. Still, somehow, they worked for his style.

He'd never worn a bowtie or cravat, but seemed to have fashioned a uniform out of a worn, off-white buttoned-up chemise and a pair of denim bib overalls. Another odd particularity about Hugo was that he'd always worn the same pair of pants. I'd known this because his one and only pair had a speck of yellow paint near the left pant leg that only I ever seemed to notice.

He'd make the effort to switch his chemise every day, but even though he'd thrown on a fresh shirt, the colors never varied too far from the bland pallet of cream, white, and off-white colors. Sometimes he'd button the shirt up tight against his Adam's apple, while other times he'd prefer to leave the collar unbuttoned, revealing several straggly looking black hairs in the deep groove of his neck.

It had always struck me as strange that Hugo, a man who'd appeared to take such great care and effort to style his mustache, would otherwise spend so little thought on the rest of his appearance, least of all, the state of his hair. He'd been clean-shaven every morning, but unyieldingly would have grown a proper five o'clock shadow by each afternoon.

His wild and unruly mop of thick, wavy black hair that looked healthy and shiny under the fluorescent bulbs hanging in the shop, but his messy head of hair had often acted as a spiderweb, catching frayed bits of loose threads, holding them prisoner until the day's work came to an end.

Hugo smiled a lot; I remember that clearly. He'd never shown any concern for the terrible state of his teeth or the fact that some molars had permanent black caps. Whenever he laughed, it was like tiny black crowns bobbing up and down.

22

He'd always been humming a tune, tapping a foot on the concrete floor of the shop. He'd worked alone and meticulously, and to the shopkeeper's dismay, he'd never appeared to be in a rush. But everyone had known that Hugo was the best at his job, so they'd let him be.

He'd seemed to enjoy his solitary work, rejoicing in making perfect seams, tightly hugging stunning fabrics over beautifully crafted furniture. Most of the time, the fabrics were specifically ordered for a project, but other times, he got to choose which ones to use. This is what he'd loved most of all.

Hugo had called himself an artist and loved having a chance to express his creativity in the colors and styles he'd offered each piece. What should have taken him a couple of weeks had often taken well over a month to complete. He'd been slow and careful, but the customers had come to know his work and had often sought him out for it.

He'd built a reputation in the town. After all, once it was covered with layers of foam and fabric, no one ever noticed the frame. The design the Upholsterer chose was what attracted buyers. Most customers would decide to buy a piece before ever sitting in it. At that point, it had simply been a bonus that the chair was well-built as well as stunning to look at. Hugo had made the sales happen, and the owners had known it. So they'd left him alone.

The way Hugo had walked around the shop had been like he'd owned it. I guess in some ways he'd kind of had.

His father had owned the shop and taught Hugo everything he'd known about the art of upholstery.

The new owners were the same ones that had purchased the business from Hugo's father, so they'd tended to treat him better than everyone else, giving him more time on projects and other, less-obvious benefits. They'd intended to keep him happy as they'd promised his father they would, back when honor and staying true to one's word actually meant something.

Hugo's father died when Hugo had been only thirteen, so the owners had taken him under their wing, taking over his care, ensuring he'd been fed, employed, and looked-after. It had been admirable and commendable of them. I don't believe too many shop owners would be willing to go the extra mile like that for their employees nowadays.

Since he'd stuck around, I'd spent several weeks with Hugo. I'd enjoyed the soft baritone of his voice as he'd sung old, French war songs he'd learned from his father. On the anniversary of his father's death, Hugo preferred to stay late at the shop. He'd grab an old bottle of whiskey he'd had stashed in a secret compartment in the wall behind some old boards and would pour himself a finger or two of the gold liquid to drain on the spot.

I'd only witnessed this once, of course, but I'd heard from the older models in the stores, those Hugo had built long before me, that he did this every year on the same day. It had been Hugo's way to remember his father but also a way to forget his pain as it often came too fast and too heavy to bear.

I hadn't expected to ever get to see it for myself.

It had been a deeply emotional and personal moment where Hugo, wanting to feel close to his father and remember him in the place they'd both loved immensely, had collapsed on the dusty concrete floor, no longer a grown man, but the young child he'd been when he'd lost his father.

The shop, in many ways, had been Hugo's home. It was where he'd felt most comfortable and nearest to his father. He'd spent most of his childhood in the back of that shop, learning everything he'd needed to know about furniture making. It was also where his interest in upholstery had been sparked.

He'd enjoyed putting the final touches on pieces that would be cherished for decades in other peoples' homes. He'd seemed to understand how a chair could impact the overall design and feel of a room. How it might eventually get associated with a loved one, or fought over for being the most comfortable seat in the house. On some level, I even think he'd understood how the chairs he'd worked on might one day hold up a weary body, console another, offer a resting place for an exhausted one, and even be used as a prop in family pictures. The possibilities were endless. And that had been what most of us in the shop looked forward to once we'd received our last staple and final inspection.

I remember the day I was displayed in the front window of the store, standing high next to a matching ottoman. Propped up on an elevation lip, I'd had the best view of the bustling street and the store floor.

From this perspective, I'd been able to observe the comings and goings of serious businessmen in dark suits, gripping tightly to important-looking and elegantly constructed briefcases. I'd watched women wearing stylish trench coats, leather gloves, and high healed knee-high boots, walking briskly by, often holding onto or coaxing a child begging for the latest toy in the shop window next door.

The furniture shop had been pretty quiet, and I'd liked it that way. I'd enjoyed watching the world pass by, entertained by the busyness and life happening just outside the windowpane, but able to appreciate and find solace in the stillness within the shop. In some ways, it had felt almost poetic since the shop hosted an assortment of furniture that encouraged these busy bodies to rest, sit around a table to share a meal, read a book, or enjoy a drink at the end of a long day.

Whatever happened out there, there we'd been, waiting for them as steady, reliable companions. We never judged, never argued, and never reproached. We were just there as silent witnesses to their lives, unwaveringly present, offering peace and reassurance. They could count on us.

CHAPTER 3

When George walked past me the first time, I'm ashamed to admit that I hadn't paid much attention to him. I'd been so distracted by a couple of squirrels fighting over a particularly appetizing looking nut in a nearby tree branch to notice him.

He'd been sauntering past on his way home, his hands shoved deeply inside of his navy-blue mechanic's uniform, his name stitched in cursive on a pocket just over his heart. His brows had been furrowed as he'd stopped abruptly before me, finally catching my attention. We'd regarded each other for a few minutes, contemplating the implications of this developing interest. His lips had moved into different shapes as he'd pondered, gazing down towards the delicately penned price-tag at my feet.

I'd noticed the rise and fall of his chest and how he'd seemed to deflate as he'd taken me in. It had been as though he'd felt relaxed just by looking at me.

He'd been so young then, his wedding ring shiny and unscratched on his finger as he'd lifted a hand to scratch his chin while he'd contemplated me. It was a mannerism I'd later come to recognize as George's deep-thinking pose.

We'd remained like this for a long time, until his gaze glossed over, and he'd caught sight of his own reflection in the glass, startling him and breaking whatever link we'd shared. He'd seemed to take himself in, letting his gaze linger on the grease smudges over his forehead and fingernails. He'd visibly hunched his shoulders as he'd offered me one last fleeting look, shuffling back into the busy street, getting swallowed up in the sea of late workers on their way home, the night falling quickly at his back.

I'd held my breath until I'd no longer been able to see him on the street. It had been a particular interaction. I'd never felt a connection to any other person who'd stopped to gaze at me through the windowpanes of the shop. I hadn't known what to expect.

The other pieces, those who'd been around longest, had told tales of customers peering through the shop's windows, some coming back week after week for a glimpse of a piece before finally stepping inside the shop to purchase it, while other customers would simply fall in love at first sight. I wasn't sure what this man's final assessment of me had been, but I'd remained hopeful for his return.

Thankfully, I hadn't had to wait long.

George had come back the very next night, a crisp check in hand, his fingers neatly scrubbed, wearing a smart-looking shirt, creaseless dark pants, and shiny black shoes. On his arms was a blond-haired woman with a severe face, pressed lips and a pointy chin, who'd seemed to be judging every element of whatever her eyes landed on. But still, I'd been overjoyed to see him return, almost not recognizing him at first. He'd strode inside the shop with quiet assurance, decidedly set on bringing me home that very evening.

That first night had been one of the happiest moments of my entire life. I'd found a home.

George's pride had been evident as he'd settled me in the living room where most of their lives happened. He'd sit in me every chance he'd get. Although it was never verbally discussed, it seemed to be a mutual agreement that I'd been purchased to be solely his chair. The woman hadn't shared the same level of enthusiasm at my comfort. Her backside had barely grazed me in an attempt to pacify George before she'd returned to her hard and padding-less rocking chair where she would sit and knit most nights.

My new owners' home was not nearly as quiet and still as George's house had been or as echoey as the furniture shop where I'd originally come from. Instead, it reminded me of the busy street I'd watched from my stoop in the shop's window.

People came and went all the time it seemed. During the week, I'd had hours to myself when my owners went to work, coming home utterly exhausted, happily collapsing on me for a short rest before resuming their evening activities. Not a spare moment was wasted with these two.

I admired their tenacity and drive. I'd been created as a symbol of luxury, a place to relax, but it had quickly become apparent to me that these two didn't know how to stop. The term work-acholic would fit well with their work ethic, but it didn't cover every element of their lives. It hadn't been just work that filled their days, but a multitude of various activities they were constantly participating in. These folks just didn't stand still for very long.

It had often crossed my mind that they'd chosen to keep busy as a way to fill a void or to add noise where there was mostly uncomfortable silence.

The room adjoining the living room remained empty for many years. The couple worked hard to save up and purchase a second-hand dining table and chairs. I'd been so happy for them when they'd finally brought it in and hosted their first proper dinner party. The house finally seemed complete.

The couple's cat, Merlot, would spend most of its time with me in those early days, taking full advantage of the perch I offered with an ideal view of the neighboring birds. The house would remain quiet during the day and a sort of peace seemed to settle over Merlot and I as we would sit in pleasant silence enjoying each other's company, each of us happily lost in our own thoughts.

I'd been surprised to develop a great affinity to Merlot's presence, except for those odd times when she'd used one of my legs as a scratch post. That part I would have gladly done without.

My cushions had gotten the brunt of it one fateful day.

Thankfully, the woman had been around the house that day and had put a stop to it before Merlot had the chance to completely destroy all of Hugo's handiwork. I'd been incredibly grateful for her quick intervention, for if it hadn't been for her, I might not have lived to see all that was to come in the following years. Which would have been a pity because so much happened—good and bad, but mostly, life happened—and I'd been glad to be around long enough to witness it.

Furniture came and went over the years, but I'd been one of the lucky pieces that remained somehow against all the odds.

They'd eventually moved me away from the window and replaced my favorite spot with a beige leather couch. They hadn't been able to withstand the social pressures of interior design and a fascination with Pinterest-inspired spaces.

That, and they'd eventually realized they needed additional seating for their many guests. I was then placed on the opposite side of the fireplace, still a desired spot, but my view of the outdoors was slightly compromised by the couch.

The distance between myself and the window made it so that I'd had to squint each time I'd wanted to gaze outdoors, causing me mild discomfort. Still, I hadn't wanted to complain about it. Mostly, I'd been glad not to have gotten discarded while many of the other pieces had changed hands without any chance of redemption, even with the craze of upcycling and chalk-painting of furniture. I'd been lucky.

Thankfully, my beautiful Queen Anne companion had remained by my side, never more than a few feet away from me. Over the years, she'd begun to warm up to my persistent and charming persona, opening up about her previous owners and her life before. Talking about her past home proved to be a difficult subject for her.

She'd been constructed and purchased as part of a set, but her identical twin hadn't been as lucky as she'd had. It too, had served mainly as a décor piece, very rarely being used as a seat, except for one unfortunate day, when an irresponsible guest spilled black coffee all over the front of it.

The priceless chair had been put to the curb the very next day. Sadly, the stain deterred anyone from bringing it home, therefore, there had been no second-chance at redemption for it. Queen Anne had watched for days as her twin sat there alone, dejected and soiled, until the day the garbage truck picked it up.

She'd witnessed, to her horror, unable to turn away, her twin being lifted in the back of a truck and crushed beneath the weight of the machine.

Talking about it, even years later, still brings tears to her eyes. She'd found it hard to get close to any other piece ever since. I'd fallen quiet when she'd told me her story. I don't think I could have moved on if I'd witnessed something as awful as she'd described.

She'd been moved to the lawn on a warm May morning, placed atop a red and white checkered picnic blanket, alongside a stunning set of freshly oiled teak coffee tables, an array of crystal bowls, and China plates.

The sidewalk had been bustling with curious shoppers and bargain hunters walking the streets of a prestigious neighbourhood in Ottawa for the famous, annual Glebe garage sale. Her home had been in the center of it, right beside the park, with a large porch to enjoy tea in the evenings and tasteful wallpaper covering each interior wall.

To go from a place like that to this home would have been quite the adjustment for anyone but she'd never complained about it. She'd been determined to make the best of her situation, putting the past behind her and choosing instead to focus on the present. Once we'd gotten to know each other a little better, the days hadn't felt quite as long.

Merlot quickly adapted to my new spot away from the window, finding comfort in my soft cushions, despite having an obstructed view of the birds. She would simply split her time between me and the top cushion of the couch.

That year, I saw so many babies come and go from the house. Smiling couples would cradle their bundle of joy, bouncing it up and down whenever they cried.

Cute, rounded cheeks that could turn a scary shade of purple as it accompanied possibly the worst sound I'd ever heard. I'd remembered this sound from my time with George, when he'd first become a grandfather.

His children, then grown adults and parents themselves, would thrust their new babies into his arms to hold, taking advantage of the fact that their father was already sitting down.

The babies in this new home were friends' babies and the man and woman loved holding them. They would coo to them and sometimes even sing to them. Families with multiple kids were regular visitors. Every other weekend, the house would be filled with toddlers running around from room to room or crawling all over me as though I'd been a jungle gym. I'd been pleased to be the source of their entertainment, but also grateful for the quiet that eventually followed once everyone left.

One time, a large group of the couples' friends had stayed well into the early morning, clinking beer bottles or glasses of wine together, wearing silly party hats, and playing board games for hours before counting backwards together to celebrate the New Year. One of the guests had fallen asleep on me and I'd felt incredibly proud to have offered him a cozy place to lay his head, even for just a few moments before he'd woken up and rejoined the festivities.

As much as the couple had seemed to enjoy the peace and quiet that came whenever everyone left, it was nearly impossible to effectively ignore the looming and uncomfortable weighted silence that would fill the house. Sadness, quickly replacing the cries of joy and stirring conversations.

Unable to do anything to change it or maybe opting to ignore the void that had become more and more apparent, the couple had done what they could. They had started filling up the physical empty spaces with material things: plants, baskets, frames for the bare walls, colorful rugs, and other matching decorations.

Unlike many others before them, the couple rather enjoyed my distinct color and had embraced it by finding matching curtains to dress the large windows. A matching teal vase was added to the fireplace mantle over time as well, often holding whatever wildflowers were in season. The color became the accent, as they often described with great pride to their many visitors. I'd offered a splash of color to the otherwise beige and gray surroundings.

In this house, my most cherished moments happened during Christmas time, as the teal seemed to morph to a deeper shade of forest green, complimenting the deep ruby reds of the stockings hanging over the fireplace and the sparkling red glass ornaments affixed to the tree. The Christmas tree would take up most of the bay window in the living room and glitter well into the evenings with thousands of tiny white lights winking through the thick foliage. The room was exquisite at that time of year. Pops of reds, silver, and green were strewn all over the space, making it cozy and festive all at once.

A red tree skirt announced *Merry Christmas*, and an assortment of hand-made or precious ornaments in various shapes, colors, and sizes were proudly displayed on the branches of the tree, topped with a sparkly silver snowflake.

With soft, white flakes of snow falling outside, the warm fire keeping me toasty warm, I'd welcomed my owners during their winter evenings with books, a warm blanket, and comforting tea, holding their tired bodies tightly until their eyes eventually grew heavy.

That had always been my favorite time of year as the couple spent almost every waking moment in the same room as me, between lounging by the fire, eating delectable meals, sipping wine, or opening shinny wrapped presents. They'd seemed to be around a lot more during this time of year, spending less of their days outdoors and more of them inside, cozied up together, finally adopting a slower pace of life, enjoying deep, meaningful conversations about dreams, or swapping fascinating stories, wrapped in thick, knitted sweaters and wool socks.

The same room always felt so large and empty whenever the holiday decorations were returned to storage boxes and to the darkness of the basement. There was an adjustment period for all of us to get used to the room without all that cheery, bright life to fill it.

The rest of the winter months dragged along in gloomy fashion, the chill lingering in the corners of each room, no matter how many logs were shoved into the fireplace cavity. The couple had been forced to make-up their own warmth and sparkle by relying on each other, focusing instead on hobbies and alternative interests.

One year, the emptiness left behind after Christmas seemed particularly hard. The couple had sat on the floor in front of the fireplace and were sobbing, holding onto each other like lifejackets during a sudden storm in the middle of an ocean.

I'd desperately wanted to offer them some semblance of comfort, but I hadn't known how to. The woman had clutched her stomach so tightly, I'd winced imaging the pain.

Tears had slid down her cheeks, grief and hopelessness seeping out as sorrow rattled inside her body without anywhere to go. The two of them had sat on the floor for most of that afternoon and through the evening.

The fire had grown cold and the man, visibly exhausted and emotionally drained, had gone upstairs to their bedroom, reluctantly leaving the woman behind.

Slowly, I'd watched over her as she'd laid down on the carpet before me, her eyes shut and puffy from crying. She'd mumbled a prayer to someone I hadn't managed to see. She'd stayed there for several hours before abruptly standing up with new resolve, seemingly leaving her grief right there on the floor. Wiping off the cat hair from her black leggings, she'd sniffled once before turning away and climbing the stairs without another word.

Things got busy again after that night. They'd seemed to be away from home more than ever before. New jobs were celebrated, and their time quickly filled up with new hobbies. They'd learned to play guitar but soon realized they were both unbelievably terrible at it, playing 'Smoke on the water' on repeat for weeks on end. Apparently, it had been the only song they'd learned how to play.

I'd been so relieved when they'd finally given that up. I still get a little weary whenever they bring out that old guitar, plucking a few familiar chords. It gives me major flashbacks of the dreaded tune.

After guitar, they'd launched themselves headfirst into photography. I'd found the fancy cameras most interesting.

The little plastic machines, so intricate, had so many particularities and small pieces, it was a wonder how they kept it all straight. There were long lenses to affix, batteries with secret compartments, memory cards to slide into an almost unnoticeable slot, an add-on flash to slide on top, and a tiny cleaning brush that was most fascinating to me. Of course, they'd started with one camera but soon purchased a second one, lacking patience to wait their turn with it and refusing to share the time with the camera equally.

On weekends, they would empty their camera bags on the coffee table in the living room and begin carefully cleaning lenses and pushing buttons to get the settings just right. Then they'd spend hours walking around the house with the cameras hanging from their necks, practicing new techniques to achieve the effects they were seeking.

Eventually, they'd built a makeshift studio in the basement. People in suits, families with tiny babies, and little girls in adorable tulle dresses would skip down the steps and have their pictures taken. Most weekends had been dedicated to this new venture, leaving very little time with me. They'd seemed to be working every day of the week during those days. I remember starting to get worried about them.

It had been obvious to me, but clearly not to them, that they'd been filling the space in their hearts, the holes created by shattered dreams, by keeping themselves so busy that they didn't have to think about the harder things. They'd hardly ever talked about that night when they'd cried by the fireplace anymore.

One day in the spring, binders and stacks of paper appeared on the coffee table. There had been a buzzing in the room. I'd just known something important had happened. The couple began dedicating so much of their time filling out these papers. They'd have long, drown-out conversations before writing anything on the papers. They'd pause to read or research something on their laptop, often disagreeing, but almost always coming to an agreement in the end. I hadn't fully been able to grasp the meaning of their strange behavior, until the day a woman with a fancy blazer and a clipboard showed up in the home and peaked around every inch of the place, inspecting every corner and jotting down whatever needed to be changed as she walked.

She'd asked them many questions. I'd begun worrying that they were planning to move, thinking the woman in the blazer was assessing the house to sell it. But I'd been wrong in the end. The woman with the clipboard had been a social worker, conducting a home study, to assess if the couple and their home were fit to adopt a baby.

The social worker had sat on me as she'd interviewed my owners. The tension in the room had been palpable, even though she'd been kind and pleasant, it had been obvious to me that the stakes had been high.

I'd been terrified to do anything to jeopardize their chances. I'd known how badly my owners wanted a child of their own, after seeing them hold all of their friends' babies over the years.

The yearning on their faces and the pain they'd experienced when they'd lost theirs had been visible in their eyes.

I'd wanted this so badly for them, but the process had been daunting, not to mention the astronomical costs involved. I'd practically seen the hope drain from their faces upon hearing this information, but to my astonishment, they hadn't backed down. Instead, they'd gotten to work, making plans, saving money in mason jars, tightening their budget. They'd confided to friends and family about their dream to adopt so that everyone was aware of their plans and wouldn't take it personally if the couple couldn't go out to dinner at restaurants or splurge like they'd once been able to. They'd been determined to cut down on non-essentials, finding alternative ways to be frugal. They'd clipped coupons, accepted second-hand clothing, renewed their library cards, started making coffee at home, and planned bigger meals that would last through the week as well as lunches they could bring to work.

They'd resolved to make it work, but the ups and downs of the journey would nearly cost them everything. I'd felt for them in those harsh months and years of waiting. As beautiful as adoption had the potential of being, the months and years of waiting in the dark were brutal and bordering on emotional torture. The hope they'd felt wavered even if they'd worked so hard not to allow it to. They'd felt the weight of the emotions in turns, never coming to it from the same place, like racers starting from different starting lines.

After months of agonizing silence and tired of the routine, they'd booked a trip, deciding to follow the advice from the social worker, choosing to live their lives rather than sit around and wait for what might never happen.

They'd only left for a week, but when they'd returned, the energy had been high and contagious.

Excited phone calls had been made, tears of joy had been shed, boxes of tiny clothing, plastic bottles, toys, and board books were delivered by friends in exchange for hugs and well-wishes.

They'd spent a lot of time upstairs right above me, moving things around, discussing layouts, paint colors, and putting shelving along with a new ceiling light in the small room.

One day, while the man was at work, the woman had painted the tiny room by herself, starting with one, then two coats. The house had smelled strongly of latex, but she hadn't seemed to feel the effects of it. Whether she'd been oblivious by the paint fumes or perhaps motivated by the fast-approaching date they'd discussed increasingly since they'd return from vacation.

Two days later, my owner received an important phone call and had nearly collapsed on the spot. She'd frozen in place, practically unable to speak, resolving to nod furiously, unknown to the caller, before she'd gratefully accepted whatever conditions had been discussed.

Rushing upstairs, I'd heard her sobbing into the phone as she'd presumably called her husband, who'd arrived home shortly after.

With haste, the couple had left the house and hadn't returned until the following night, this time, with a beautiful little baby girl all bundled tightly in their arms.

CHAPTER 4

The precious girl was squirmy and red-faced when she'd arrived. The couple had fussed over her, dropping bags of diapers, an array of blankets, photo albums, plastic bottles of water, fast-food wrappers, and a thick folder filled with documents all over the living room floor. They'd shed their coats one after another, passing the child between them, taking turns kissing the top of her fuzzy head. The baby, already a month old, had a fluffy crown of golden hair that would have no doubt tickled my nose.

The woman's parents arrived minutes later, knocking softly at the door as though trying not to disturb them, even though all the lights had been turned on indoors. Despite it being the middle of the night, the new grandparents had arrived bright-eyed, with wide smiles stretched across their faces.

Never taking their eyes off the now-settled bundle nestled in the woman's arms, they'd quickly shaken the snow from their coats, wiped their boots on the entrance rug and abandoned their winter armor by the door. They'd hesitantly, but excitedly entered further into the house, never breaking eye-contact with their daughter, gazing at her with pride and pure happiness. Hugs and congratulations had been exchanged as tears had brimmed in everyone's eyes. They'd all kept their voices hushed, not wanting to disturb the baby. It had been obvious to me how much restraint it had taken for the new grandparents not to jump with joy.

The only sounds in the house had been the distant tick of the kitchen clock and the soft murmurs of the adults congregating around the baby. My owners had driven nine hours in a severe winter storm, stopping only twice along the way for gas, food, and a diaper change at the man's mother's house along the way.

The couple recounted the day with the social workers and foster parents, the scary drive home, smiling and crying with joy. They'd been exhausted but unbelievably happy. When the baby had begun squirming in her arms, the woman had offered her mother the opportunity to bottle-feed her daughter. The emotion on the newly appointed grandmother had been evident as she'd sat down on me so quickly that she'd almost bounced right off. Once settled in her seat, she'd raised her arms to welcome and meet her granddaughter.

Tears had been flowing freely in the room by this point and it had taken everything in me to hold it together.

I'd felt so honored to be a part of this intimate moment and to play such an important role in creating this core memory.

The couple had taken pictures as both grandparents huddled together around me to get a closer look at the baby and gush over her. I'd become a staple in their family pictures and the envy of my dear Queen Anne, who had hoped and failed to be the first one to get the chance to hold the baby.

Getting to witness this special moment had immediately reminded me of the times I'd met George's grandchildren, however, I'd never gotten to see them quite as little as that baby girl.

George's children had only brought their kids over months after their birth, opting to delay the trip to George's house, until they'd had the chance to get settled in their new routines and only after the babies had been vaccinated. That freezing winter night had been my very first look at a new baby.

The privilege had delighted me. I'd taken in her tiny fingers, wiggly toes, and marveled at the details in the fingernails and eyelashes. She'd been so new, so perfect. She'd made the cutest noises when she'd drank from the bottle and had everyone enchanted.

I'd found it hard not to giggle at the way her nose scrunched up whenever she'd stifled a yawn or adjusted her mouth over the nipple of the bottle. I'd relished the time spent with her as well as the quiet moments where I'd had a great view of her and could observe her to my heart's content.

Over the next few years, I'd gotten to watch her grow-up into an energetic and lively toddler.

She'd loved climbing over my arms and jumping down, not seeming to mind or be aware of the potential dangers or the height. She'd been fearless and loud, but undeniably wonderful. Her laugh had been contagious from the start and her imagination limitless.

She would spend her days dragging around an assortment of stuffed animals everywhere she went, interchanging them along the way. Only one seemed to always remain by her side at all times—a little lamb she loved above all the other animals.

It had once been covered with a beautiful, fluffy, white coat, but now had visible signs of aging, its fur matted, greyed, and bumps from where stitches had reattached an arm and its neck on multiple occasions. But did she ever love that lamb! It went with her everywhere and God-forbid she ever lost him in the house somewhere. Bedtime would become a battlefield whenever that was the case, no matter how diligently her parents tried to keep tabs on the whereabouts of the beloved lamb, it always seemed to find new places to hide.

From my vantage point, I'd usually be able to spot it hiding beneath the couch or feel it wedged snuggly between my cushion and frame, but there hadn't been much I'd been able to do to alert them of its hiding spot. They'd eventually discover it and all would be right in the little girl's world once more.

Being situated in the living room, I'd quickly become the main attraction for her to play. If she wasn't climbing me, she'd be expertly removing my seat cushion and tossing it onto the ground along with Queen Anne's, pretending the floor was lava. She would jump from one cushion to the other with the goal of making it across the room unharmed.

She'd play this game for hours and weeks in a row, never bothering to put the cushions back when finished, leaving that task to her mother.

Other times, she'd propped my cushion up against Queen Anne's to make an inverted V and had draped a large blanket over us, pretending to be exploring a cave. For a year, around her third birthday, she'd built forts almost every morning, playing in them for the better part of the day. She'd hosted tea parties for her dolls, pretended to read to her stuffed animals, and ate snacks under the comfort of her creative enclosure.

The family cat, growing jealous and impatient by all the attention I'd been receiving from the little girl, took it out on me one day, reclaiming the damage it had begun years previously. Using my legs as a scratching post, she'd left permanent damage to the wood and to Hugo's beautiful work. I hadn't been able to fault Merlot for being resentful. The poor cat was all but ignored around there in those days. The couple had been so busy caring for their daughter that they'd barely had time for anything else.

Thankfully for me, the scratches had only been visible on my left side, therefore I'd been able to maintain my position beside the fireplace without embarrassing my owners with my fresh scars.

To their credit, they'd tried their very best to fix me up, rubbing oils on my scratches, attempting to sew up any newly ripped pieces of fabric, but none of it had managed to return me to my perfect state. They hadn't had the skills, or the tools that Hugo had had. It had also become apparent to everyone, including myself, that I'd been quickly becoming a rather old chair.

They'd brought in new furniture over the years and even though I'd managed to remain a favourite, I'd inevitably become one of their oldest pieces. Unfortunately, they just didn't seem to care for me the same way they'd once had when they'd first brought me home all those years before.

They'd had a lot to concern themselves with and a young child to chase all throughout the house. But still, it had been impossible not to notice the neglect bestowed upon me ever since the new baby had arrived.

I hadn't necessarily been jealous. No, it hadn't been that. What I'd felt had been a sort of dreaded disappointment that slowly came to fruition—one that maybe I should have anticipated but that had sprung on me a lot faster than I'd imagined. Even so, the brutal reality of my impending predicament had stung.

I'd seen this kind of forgetfulness and neglect happen time and time again whenever a new piece of furniture would be wished for, saved up for, shopped for, cherished, and admired, until the next new piece was desired.

Unfortunately for me, humans seemed to offer affections out like candy on Halloween, jumping from one piece to another, tossing out what no longer worked with every new spark of design inspiration. It is rare to see a piece of furniture remain in a home for even a decade nowadays. I guess I should have considered myself lucky that they'd held on to me even if they barely used me anymore. I'd become a part of the background. No longer the shiny new chair, but just part of the room, as though I had always been there.

One evening, my owners' friend spilled the contents of a glass of red wine all over one of my arms, staining the fabric. The liquid seeped quickly into me and I'd unwillingly absorbed the alcohol making me feel a lightness I'd never experienced before or since. It had tickled me to no end when they'd furiously dabbed a wet rag over the stain, trying to soak up remaining liquid, desperate to remove stains, hoping to save me from untimely ruin.

Unfortunately for me, I'd never been viewed quite the same way after that. I think that was around the time the woman came home with a brand-new wingback chair that smelled of plastic and fabric softener.

She hadn't replaced me, per-say—she'd never even moved me from my spot—but it had been apparent to me that she'd preferred this new, slate grey chair to my cat-fur and wine infused coating.

Every evening, she would cuddle up in that new chair with a book, facing me, almost like she'd done so on purpose, perhaps to make me jealous by wordlessly taunting me to speak up regarding the sudden unfairness of her unwarranted rejection.

The fact that she'd so blatantly deceived me had made me bitter and furious, but I'd somehow managed to stamp down my hurt by reminding myself over and over that I'd never appeared in her life with the sole purpose of becoming her favorite chair but mainly with the goal of being a constant presence, one she could rely on.

I'd opted to shut my eyes to the pain, ignoring the scene that regularly unfolded before me and had vowed to remain loyal despite the injustice of growing older.

I'd been around far longer than this Allan-key, want-to-be, boring grey chair, and I'd intended to stick around for the long-haul. I'd felt better allowing myself to believe that this new fling of hers wouldn't last and that one day soon, she'd come back to me.

CHAPTER 5

For a long while, I'd remained in the same spot. Forgotten, or rather, replaced, I'd kept company with old, discarded boardgames, who'd succumbed to the same fate as me, gathering dust on a shelf beneath the coffee table.

On those long, dreadful days, I'd regularly distract myself by watching spiders develop impressive webs in the corners of the crown molding. The delicate structures would grow more detailed and beautiful with each passing day. Queen Anne and I would spend hours silently listening to the faraway giggles of the growing toddler as she'd run around in her newly appointed playroom in the basement—the photography studio long since replaced by bright, plastic toys, some so large they'd barely fit down the steps.

The family spent most of their days down there back then, only ever coming up for air for the occasional snack before submerging themselves downstairs once more. They'd resurface from the basement and back into our vicinity so rarely, that I'd had no other choice but to find other ways to entertain myself.

One spring night, I made friends with the thousands of mosquitos that entered through the fireplace, surprising both myself and my owners. It had taken quite a while for the couple to notice them. The tiny bloodsuckers had taken full advantage of having free-range of the place, sniffing my owners out all the way to the other end of the house.

At first, I'd heard slaps and groans coming from the rec room as the couple, presumably slouched on the sofa, had started growing impatient at the constant and increasing buzzing in their ears. I'd heard the woman complain, followed by the familiar creak of her body as she'd stood from her spot on the couch to investigate. I'd listened intently to the slow shuffle of her feet as she'd made her way over to me.

By then, the room had been buzzing with the tiny insects, flying all over the place with no apparent destination. There were some casually resting upside-down on the ceiling and others gripping tightly to the curtains, trying to camouflage themselves within the design. A few more daring ones had flown right beside her face as she'd swatted at them. She'd managed to catch a few but it had soon become obvious that there were more mosquitos than she'd be able to manage on her own.

Fearing defeat, she'd called out to her husband for assistance. For the following two hours, Queen Anne and I had been enthusiastically entertained by our owners as they'd mercilessly swatted, smashed, and decimated my new friends. They'd eventually resolved to greater measures and had decided to capture them in a duct-taped, hand-held vacuum. Within minutes of turning on the device, the room was cleared of all mosquitoes and returned to its usual calm status.

I can still remember how the gathering of the buzzing insects trapped within the confines of the plastic canister had created a surprisingly loud and constant pinging noise as the frantic insects failed to find a way out.

The couple had made quick work of securing a large, plastic garbage bag over the opening of the fireplace to ensure no more mosquitos could enter their home, affixing duct tape to any potential opening, therefore ensuring that no more intruders could penetrate their personal space.

They'd seemed satisfied with their handywork, comparing the redness of their palms, and laughing in defeat at all the insect guts had smeared all over their otherwise pristine walls. Ultimately, understandably exhausted, they'd returned to their resting spot at the opposite end of the house, leaving us once more in the dark loneliness.

It had been quite the show and I'd enjoyed seeing so much action happening all around me. The mosquitos had never bothered me, so I'd deeply felt the emptiness of their absence for the following week as the blocked fireplace failed to produce any more unexpected visitors.

Eventually, the bag was removed and new visitors, hornets this time, began flying around the room as though they'd owned the place. To the woman's distress, they hadn't been quite as subtle as the mosquitos had been, nor had they been as shy or evasive either, often giving her a scare, especially when they'd flown angrily around her daughter.

The yellow assault weapons always seemed so angry with them and would chase the pair around the house as though they'd had targets on their backs.

For whatever reason, the hornets would often congregate in the front windows of the living room. Every day, without fail, there would be one buzzing there, intently banging its head against the pane of glass, calling attention to itself in a frantic manner the woman couldn't ignore. She'd been merciless with those creatures.

To me, the hornets had simply been lost and scared, never intending to cause anyone any harm, but simply trying to find their way back to the outdoors. Unfortunately for them, they'd been no match for the horribly toxic product the woman would spray over them, squeezing the trigger for so long that it coated their wings, and bodies generously, not allowing a shred of doubt that they'd ever make a full recovery. The only solace was that the insects would die withing seconds of the spray hitting them, so I'd never have to watch them suffer for long.

I'd been able to tell by the way her nose would scrunch up and how quickly she'd exit the room, that the strong smell bothered her. She would avoid inhaling it, anxious of the notorious ingredients powerful enough to kill on contact.

But I'd had no choice but to remain rooted in my spot, taking in the chemicals and watching the hornets twist and die before me. They're drying carcasses would remain on the windowsill for days, allowing me a front-row seat to observe its hardening corpse curl and shrink over time.

For the most part, my owners seemed like genuinely good, kind-hearted people. They cared about their family and friends, but doom loomed over you if you were an insect. I'd never appreciated being a chair more, even if I'd go days being ignored. It had seemed better than getting their full attention only to be terminated on the spot. It hadn't mattered if the bugs were harmless, flying, or crawling, if it had the bad luck of running into their path, they were as good as gone.

Over the weeks that followed, there came a new visitor. I knew it was an important person because of the way the woman tended to me. I'd receive a full vacuum, a rarity that left me feeling inexplicably naked. Even the long-ago forgotten crumbs under my pillow seat were sucked up, along with the ever-present accumulation of cat hair that seemed to weave itself within the fibers of my cushion cover. I'd then been sprayed with a light, but pleasant scent that reminded me of rain. She'd even gone through the trouble of fluffing my seat.

Later that same afternoon, I'd welcomed an older, more fragile woman who'd carefully settled on me, slowly lowering herself, placing her wooden cane against one of my armrests. She'd weighed practically nothing, but her presence in the room had been of evident importance.

The older woman had appeared to capture everyone's attention as they'd rushed back and forth from the kitchen, holding mugs of freshly brewed coffee, delicious, flaky-looking pastries, a plate of neatly arranged cubes of cheese, crackers, and an assortment of berries.

The toddler had been almost four years old by then and she'd taken great care to dress herself in her favourite and fanciest dress. Her long golden hair had spilled down her back in a perfectly straight curtain. Her parents had undoubtfully gone through great pains to brush out the many knots, a regular issue in those days.

It had shocked me to see her looking so put-together. When had this little toddler grown-up into a little girl? I wasn't sure how I'd managed to miss it. That day, she'd surprised me by sitting remarkably still, waiting patiently for her turn to speak, in total control of herself. She'd locked her hands together as though she'd been instructed to.

I remember how her dress had been free of stains and how her beady eyes had paid close attention to the conversation happening around her, as though she'd been able to understand and retain what had been discussed. She'd further impressed me when she'd contributed to the exchange, answering questions and even offering interesting anecdotes. She'd spoken beautifully and clearly, which had appeared to impress the old woman.

When it had come time for the little girl to go up to bed, the couple had gone up to give her a bath and read her usual three bedtime stories.

The old woman had remained put, sitting with me in comfortable silence, casually staring out the window at the darkening sky. She'd been seated there for hours but hadn't appeared to grow restless. If anything, I remember feeling her getting even more comfortable. Taking full advantage of the unexpected solitude, she'd leaned her body slightly to the right and carefully let out a steady, yet silent fart, startling me, forcing me to contain a giggle.

She'd made no noise keeping her actions a secret to the rest of the household, maintaining her upstanding appearance in check and unstained, but I'd known. Having knowledge of something my owners did not had exhilarated me far more than perhaps it ought to have. It had felt like a shared confidence—a secret between us that no one else had been privy to.

It had been quite a while since someone had trusted me like this and I'd reveled in the experience. The woman had stayed for only a couple of nights before she'd left again. I'd missed her presence instantly as the room had returned once again to the regular desolate state after her departure.

The family had appeared to have little use for me after that. They'd spent most of their time in other rooms of the house. The toys the little girl had once stashed under the coffee table had since been stored in other rooms, where I'd been able to hear her play, but not watch.

Joyful noises would come from the tiny room upstairs in the early mornings as the little girl would spring out of bed, excited for another day. She'd run down the dark hallway towards her parents' room to wake them up.

She'd always been full of energy, enthusiastically leading them down the stairs, pulling on their hands, loquaciously talking to her groggy-looking parents as they'd stumbled slowly behind her, doing their best not to trip on their own feet, rubbing their crusty eyes.

Life fell into a sort of rhythm, one I got to know and expect. Time went by and to my surprise, I remained. That is, until everything changed.

CHAPTER 6

One day in the middle of the month of March, a cold snap brought along an unfamiliar energy to the household. The seriousness of the situation seemed to seep into the very fabric of my chair until I'd begun feeling queasy by it. It had been nearly impossible to ignore the tension and the worried faces of the family.

They'd spoken in hushed tones, researching information on their phones, calling friends and family on video chat, discussing ideas and activities. They'd remained in the house all the time, very rarely venturing out. It had been strange and unsettling, to say the least.

Whereas the young girl had been going to school for most of the week, she'd then been situated in front of a computer, her shoulders slumped, visibly disengaged and bored.

Tiny, square faces would fill the screen before her, but she never got to hear their voices. Her joyful energy was quickly replaced by a solemn and worrisome one that caused her parents to doubt certain decisions.

Many conversations were had in quiet corners of the house in hushed tones, seemingly afraid of the words bouncing off the walls and landing in the wrong ears. Difficult choices caused rifts between family members and made the home a difficult place to share varying views.

Medical masks had come into the house by the box, in both adult and kid sizes. Test tubes with long nasal wands were regularly extracted from rectangular carboard boxes and laid out over tables like an operating table. Heated arguments had no place to burn off any steam, so instead they'd lingered in the confines of the room corners, sticking to the walls and ceiling, waiting for the opportunity to pounce on an unexpected passerby, hovering in the shadows just waiting to ruin someone's day.

The little girl, struggling to remain seated still for long stretches of time had become reckless, angry, and destructive. Her moods would sour the whole house and it became apparent to everyone that things couldn't continue on this way.

The laptop was put away and the woman took over her daughter's education, taking a more hands-on approach. She included morning and afternoon outdoor times, practical skills, and a portion on household chores. The pair quickly regained their bond and joyful companionship that they'd spent years establishing, returning the house to a comfortable state of peace.

The girl learned useful life-skills such as folding laundry, sewing, vacuuming, and dusting. Her mother also taught her how to prepare dough and knead it into a ball, then allowing it to rise over night. The smell of fresh baked bread would fill the home every single morning and bring broad smiles of gratitude to their faces.

They'd learned new recipes every day, using whatever ingredients they'd had in the downstairs pantry. Sometimes, the strange assortment of ingredients served as inspiration, offering them agency to experiment and try meals they otherwise wouldn't have ever attempted in the past.

In a strange way, remaining at home had offered them more opportunities and quality time than ever before. The usual rush of a crammed schedule was quickly discarded and replaced with a slower, more enjoyable lifestyle.

They tried new things, used their resources, tended to their gardens, fixed up their home, made mistakes, talked more, and laughed more. Their time spent together brought me such joy. I'd loved hearing their conversations and how tenderly the girl and her mother would work around each other, how patient the mother had been with her teachings, letting the house get messy from time to time, knowing there'd be plenty of time to clean up later on. I'd practically seen the anxiety drain from her eyes as the pace of her days slowed down to a crawl.

I'd heard from the video calls she'd had with friends that not everyone seemed to be coping as well as their family had, struggling with working from home and the uncertainty of what might be coming.

Family members fought over what was right or wrong, with pressures from employers making things difficult and confusing. Many took that time to reevaluate what they wanted from life. Some even ended their marriages. The unusual circumstances had allowed them to shed light on otherwise unspoken issues, making them impossible to ignore.

Plans were put on hold, while others forged ahead, deciding to view the recent challenges as something to be surmounted. My owners had seemed happy to remain steady in their habits, managing their household on less but filling it with more abundance than ever before.

For months, I never saw anyone but the three of them and Merlot roaming about the rooms. They'd been content with this quieter version of the life they'd once led. For the most part, my owners had been some of the few to benefit from the world coming to an abrupt halt by a pandemic. They rather enjoyed their new, simpler routine.

They'd taken care of themselves, their home, fixed broken objects, relied on their own knowledge, focused on reusing and refurbishing things rather than running to the stores to purchase new items.

They'd found a renewed interest in baking and growing their own food, spending most of the summer leaning about the variety of vegetables they'd grown in their gardens. The grass had always been cut, scuffs painted over, floors had been swept, and beds regularly washed.

Smiles, laughs, and lovingly prepared meals became a regular occurrence. Whereas most people had held their breath due to fear and uncertainty, life at home had felt like a breath of fresh air.

Things had tipped back towards a more stable calmness I'd begun to appreciate and rely on. It might not have seemed like much, but the balance of it had offered some peace in knowing what was to come, allowing me to better predict the days ahead.

I'd manage to find happiness in the mundane, appreciating even the smallest of things. I'd found joy in simply peering out the window and delighted in hour-long marathons of longingly starring at Queen Anne.

My days had been simple but happy.

Life had remained like that for a long while until, unpredictably, everything changed overnight as the family grew by four paws.

CHAPTER 7

The first few weeks with the new puppy were an accumulation of chaotic moments, difficult to pry apart. There had seemed to be no order remaining in the house. Everything I'd come to expect during my days had suddenly vanished and been replaced with utter nonsense.

The dog, affectionately named Shiraz, had not been much larger than Merlot at the time, and had entered the home hesitantly at first, but had quickly grown comfortable in her new space.

She'd excitedly sprinted throughout the entire place, unaware of the strength her tiny body already held. Spotting Merlot, the dog had sprinted up the staircase in a full chase, terrifying the owners that the puppy would mistakenly take the cat for a chew toy.

In those first weeks and months, the owners regularly took Shiraz out to allow her to do her business. Whether or not it had been freezing cold, snowing, pouring rain, day or night, they'd stand out there like idiots, staring at the dog's behind, begging it to swiftly accomplish its mission. They'd sometimes be outside in the middle of the night, holding on tightly to a leash pulled so taunt, that it would sometimes cause them to lose their balance. I had not envied the new responsibilities that accompanied raising a new puppy. It had simply seemed tedious to me.

A few too many times, I'd come too close for comfort at being mistaken for a fresh patch of grass, thankfully opting for the carpeted flooring instead to relieve herself. This action always caused everyone in the household to spring into action, leaping from the couch, ready to bring Shiraz outside for the second, sometimes third pee that would surely follow. I'd been fascinated by the sheer amount of urine the small puppy held in that tiny bladder of hers. She'd seemed to always need to go in those earlier months.

For a long while, the owners hadn't understood how badly Shiraz needed to release pent-up energy. Unfortunately, they'd learned the hard way in the expanse of ripped fabrics and chewed through toys. It had been a little bit like having a baby in the house again.

Baby gates had gone up one day after a terrifying incident involving a knife left too close to the edge of the counter, just in the dog's reach. Thankfully, the woman had managed to pry the knife out of the dog's clenched teeth, corralling it in a smaller corner of the kitchen, without anyone sustaining any injuries.

The close call had been a cause of great stress, and no one wanted a repeat, hence, the barricades going up all over the place. Doors were shut to minimize access and outdoor time was prioritized.

Still, despite all of the precautions that had been put in place, the dog had made quick work of tearing things apart the moment its owners turned around or left the house. They'd begun trusting her only for that trust to be quickly broken after the family couch took the brunt of a rage attack and lost the majority of its stuffing.

In comparison, I'd managed to escape with only a minor scuff. The bottom of my seat had been ripped open, leaving my buttocks exposed to the cooling breeze of the impending fall. I'd been more embarrassed than hurt. The flapping fabric had never quite been the same after that. The edges of the bottom never reached the other side again; therefore, I'd remained in this damaged condition ever since.

I had felt resentful of her after that day, but it hadn't lasted long, for she, too, found me to be the most comfortable seat in the house and often rested on me.

Her head would lay over one of my armrests, one eye always blinking open at any whisper of movement or noise. She'd always be at the ready, never wanting to miss anything.

For a small puppy, she'd grown quickly into a medium-sized dog. The owners described her to friends and family as an American bulldog terrier. She'd been skinny and fit, with impressive muscles and a barrel of a chest.

Shiraz had a hard face that put off most visitors and a bark that made people instinctively step back, but she would lick anyone to death before using her teeth. Those, I quickly learned, she reserved for squeaky toys, blankets, and potato chips. They'd stood no chance.

I'd watched in complete amazement as her demeanor transformed over the years into a rather calm and pleasant adult dog. The owners had learned to prioritize the outdoors, allowing her to roam around, sniff to her liking, and make the most of their large property, effectively burning out some of her energy.

They'd take her with them for long car rides and family excursions, sometimes lasting most of the day. The dog had been so happy to be taken along for the ride and seemed to be on her best behavior upon their return. She and the little girl quickly became best friends, spending all of their spare time together.

Whenever the girl was at school and the owners were out of the house, it was just Shiraz, Merlot, and I in that room. We'd spend a lot of time together, soaking up the rays of sunshine, watching the birds and squirrels on the deck, or gazing at the deer and wild turkeys that would sometimes cross the lawn.

We never needed much but I'd been grateful for her company. She hadn't smelled like George's dog, Rosco had. Shiraz was a rather clean dog, and to everyone's surprise, a calm mannered one once she got over the puppy stage.

My owners developed routines and tricks that helped them adapt to life with a dog. Having never owned one in the past, it was an adjustment for them.

I don't think they'd fully grasped the full scope of what being a dog-owner entailed. I would have warned them if I'd managed to, but I hadn't known how. I'd born no markings on me from my time with Rosco since the dog training had spared me that humiliation. I hadn't been as fortunate this time. My new owners had been too slow on the draw, waiting until much of their possessions went to the curb before surrendering to a more structured form of training.

The improvement was felt almost overnight. With the entire household on board, Shiraz quickly became well-mannered, learning quickly how to behave in a way that warranted her tasty treats. The liver squares smelled absolutely foul to me, but she was always visibly delighted to see them, so I'd chosen to ignore the stench, not wanting to make her feel bad about her choice of snacks—she had enough troubles to concern herself with.

Since Shiraz became part of the family during a time where they'd been isolating from almost anyone and everyone, the dog hadn't yet learned how to behave around others. The owners also hadn't learned how to introduce her to visitors. Therefore, whenever guests arrived, it was complete madness.

All the training exercises and whatever progress had been achieved in the weeks prior would fly out the window. There would be peeing on floors, jumping on visitors, barking, excited tail wags that were surprisingly painful to the legs, and a certain obsession with biting the socks right off of people's feet. Gloves, mittens, and pompom hats would succumb to the same fate as the couch, often getting shred to pieces before anyone had the chance to reclaim them.

Many items of clothing were wrecked in those first few years until things settled down and boundaries were established.

Despite the wagging tail and the happy grunts she would omit, Shiraz also struggled with anxiety whenever the family would leave the home. She would cry and be miserable for hours until they returned. Whereas I'd gotten used to their comings and goings, always knowing they'd return at some point, even if I never knew exactly where they'd gone or how long they'd be, experience had taught me that no matter what, they always came back.

The dog however, hadn't been around long enough to learn this pattern and therefore, she would panic every single time she spotted one of them putting on their shoes, often grabbing the matching one and running off with it as an attempt to stall their departure or prevent them from leaving.

She dreaded being left alone, always wanting to be near one of them. I could relate to this feeling of missing out or fearing to be out of their sight and consequently forgotten. Still, overtime, I'd learned to appreciate this time of solitude with my thoughts. There were benefits to spending time in your own company. I happened to do my best thinking then. Having everyone around me made it difficult to nail down my different ideas, so whenever they'd leave and the house plunged into silence, I'd escape back into my mind and spend hours there.

Knowing the family would eventually return had eased most of the uncertainty and fear that had once plagued me. I'd tried explaining this to Shiraz, but she was always too upset that I doubt any of my comforting words got through to her.

Unsure of how else to ease her fears, I'd hold her shaking body until she'd eventually get so exhausted that she'd fall asleep. These micro naps weren't as restful as the other, longer naps she'd have when everyone was home. They were nerve-wracking, with sporadic movements, kicks, whines, eye-twitching, and restless muscles. It was her body's way of shutting down out of necessity to protect her sensitive mind, an attempt to force her to forget her troubles and escape for a while, or at least until her owners returned. It broke my heart to see her like this, but no amount of soothing ever seemed to help.

To add to the chaos of the household, the couple decided to begin ripping out the flooring of their main level on Christmas day of all days. They'd barely gotten rid of the decorative wrapping paper, giftbags, and boxes when the furniture was moved from the family room and crammed into the kitchen before the carpet was getting pulled up.

The house had been filled with clouds of dust for weeks. Planks of mismatched hardwood, sheets of linoleum, and rolls of carpet had been ripped out and piled outside in the accumulating snow. Drills, nail guns, saws, and heavy work boots made a resounding racket throughout the house, displacing any surviving furniture throughout the rest of the unaffected rooms.

I ended up separated from Queen Anne for the better part of a year, spending my days in a darkened, underutilized guest room, where my sole visitor happened to be the family cat. Preferring me to the soft duvet cover, I'd once again gotten the honor of offering Merlot a place to rest, accumulating a thick layer of fur on my seat cushion.

Those months spent without any interaction with the family had been brutal. I'd missed Queen Anne terribly and also strongly wished to read with the woman again. Hell, I'd even wanted to spend time with Shiraz. It had felt like I'd been unjustly punished. Those months had been miserable and lonely.

The enforced confinement had been nothing like the solitude I'd learned to enjoy in previous years. My new reality had simply felt awful. The days had seemed to stretch out like taffy, the daylight bleeding into darkness. The passage of time had blurred, becoming undefined.

I'd desperately craved interaction and distraction from boredom. There were only so many times one could count the specks on the ceiling before it brought on madness. I'd started feeling melancholic, wistfully longing for days past. Without any indication of things ever returning to their normal state, and with the main floor in complete disarray, it had been difficult to remain positive.

A litterbox was added to the room sometime later and I'd felt the stench of urine and shit permeate towards me with a ferocity I hadn't managed to avoid no matter how long I'd held my breath. I just hadn't been able to escape it.

The dust from litter particles had floated around the room and settled on me, mixing in with the ever-present cat hair, accumulating on my cushions. I'd never felt so repulsive. I'd finally meet the fate I'd come to expect from George's children, but it had hurt even more.

The love and appreciation I'd received from my new owners had led me to believe that I'd always be cherished by them.

And yet, here I'd been, discarded with other unused furnishings and décor that were years out of style in a room that was all but forgotten. The light almost never got turned on in there and the space seemed to repulse all of those who were brave enough to peer into it.

From that new location, I hadn't had a good view of the backyard, therefore I had to entertain myself by watching the light change in the sky. I'd caught sight of the odd bird flying over the roof or of a brave squirrel who had tempted fate and climbed the eavesdrop like their little paws were super-glued to it. Otherwise, my days had been filled with nothingness.

My one leg had resumed leaking out dirty, brown glue, staining the carpet. My backside hadn't yet been repaired and had left me feeling vulnerable under Merlot's curious stare as it strolled beneath me to access the rest of the house.

Unlike me, the cat had the choice to come and go as it pleased. I never would have guessed that I'd one day be in such a low frame of mind that I'd find myself envying an animal with a bad temper that enjoyed licking its own backside, but there I'd been.

Hope and light had all but deserted me. My owners had abandoned me to the dusty room. I'd become obsessed with the passage of time, counting down the minutes until the sky would once again fill with stars. It had been the only time of the day when I'd forget where I was and the predicament I'd found myself in. And for those few fleeting moments, before a cloud would cover the tiny diamonds in the sky, I'd been able to breathe a little easier.

CHAPTER 8

Months went by like this and I'd felt myself getting deeper into the darkness, like the weight of the dust and cat hair covering every inch of me was holding me down.

Occasionally, the little girl had snuck into the room and turned on the lamp, casting a yellow glow over the room. There had been a large mirror leaning on the wall on the other side of the bed and she'd carry a beautiful golden box filled with hair accessories, dropping several headbands and clips along the way, before plopping herself down in front of the mirror to work on her hair.

She would spend a long time adjusting a hair piece, trying on a variation of sparkly, plastic, or fabric headbands, working stubbornly with elastics to try and make braids in her long hair.

She'd bring hairbrushes and try her best to get all the knots out, her arms aching by the end. I'd lived for these stolen moments in her company.

Her presence and her determination to keep trying to get the perfect ponytail or braid had made me want to stick around for another day. I'd looked forward to seeing her walk through the door with her creative outfits, changing two, three, sometimes four times a day.

She had loved trying on clothes and changing her hair according to her mood. Her quiet presence had sustained me, staving off the loneliness for a short while. She would sometimes chatter to her reflection or sing a song she'd learned at school. It became a sort of ritual for us.

Every morning, the pitter patter of little feet would make their way over to the room, where I'd been waiting with anticipation. The little girl's shadow would appear in the glow of the rising sun, bringing joy and hope with her. Her tiny, outstretched arms would turn on the lamp and she'd settle onto the carpet crossed-legged before beginning her tedious work of teaching herself how to manage her wild mane.

She'd had a natural part in her hair that made one side thicker than the other. She'd struggled with this unevenness, the thicker side tending to droop lower than the thinner side. She'd grow easily frustrated but she'd been persistent.

I'd admired her tenacity fiercely. She'd taught me a little bit about who I wanted to be and how quickly I'd all but given up on a good thing.

One day, after furiously twisting the hair elastic around strands of hair, she'd paused, her hands still raised and beamed so big that it had put the glow of the lamp to shame. She'd finally done it.

She'd jumped up from the floor and raced down the stairs to share the exciting news that she now knew how to do her own hair. It had been a beautiful, joyful moment. All of her hard work had finally paid off. No one deserved more praise.

Watching her not give up on her dreams to do her own hair had helped me hope for a better future for myself. It occurred to me that possibly I wouldn't always be stuck in this room by myself with the sporadic and at times unwanted feline visitor. Just like the little girl, I rationalized that maybe, if I stuck it out a little longer, my luck would eventually change.

And then it had.

I'd been moved to the master bedroom, joining the grey wingback chair, who'd turned out to be quite likable. We'd spent a few months together in that room, swapping stories. Turns out she'd been quite knowledgeable for a young chair. She'd told me tales of huge factories and store floors built into a sort of maze, causing buyers to panic whenever they'd attempt to leave.

She'd told me of glossy white tiles stretching for miles, of warehouses filled with metal shelving, holding row after row of large cardboard boxes that housed brand spanking new pieces of furniture customers would later assemble themselves at home.

How trucks and trolleys would come and go from the warehouse, like bees in the spring.

She'd claimed that no matter how full the place was with items, she'd still been able to make-out an echo throughout the building and feel the ground shake as hundreds of people wondered about, seeking the right addition to their home.

Hearing her stories had made me shudder. She might have looked new and modern, but she hadn't been unique like me. There had literally been thousands upon thousands of copies made of her all over the world. She'd been so new that she hadn't ever had a previous owner. She'd hardly known anything about the outside world, having been built in this very house. Her experience of the world had been so limited that I'd felt sorry for her.

My jealousy had evaporated with every tale of mass production, of stacking boxes over one another, of never seeing the light of day or the birds until she'd been brought here. What a sad life that would have been.

Suddenly, my year-long isolation experience hadn't seemed quite so bad. I'd mattered to so many, that I'd felt ashamed to have taken it for granted. The grey chair had put this in perspective for me.

When the day finally came that the man lifted me up in his arms and carried me down the stairs, I'd simply smiled, ready for whatever fate was in store for me. With the front door in sight, I'd been certain that I'd be heading for the curb.

After all these years, surely, they would have no more use for an old chair like me. They'd lived their lives, updated their home, and grown their family.

The new floors had looked warm and welcoming as my owner glided over them.

To my astonishment, he'd turned at the last moment, walking away from the front door and bringing me towards the front living room. He'd placed me gently on the brand-new floor and carefully placed rubber disks beneath my legs so that I wouldn't leak all over the new floor.

I'd been speechless. I hadn't been able to fully grasp what had happened to me. After all this time, thinking I'd been abandoned, they'd planed to bring me back to my favorite spot beside the large bay window. The icing on the cake was when the man returned holding my beloved Queen Anne and set her on the other end of the window in perfect view. I'd shaken with joy. All was right again.

Eventually, a Christmas tree had gone up between us, but that hadn't stopped us from chatting the night away, recounting the last year and how grateful we both were to be back in the room where it had all started. We'd been so glad to be back in our element, taking in all the smells, the colors, and noises. It had been glorious.

It later occurred to me that my worth had not been measured by the ones who'd made me or even how well-built I'd been, but rather, by how fiercely and unconditionally I'd been cherished by those who'd loved me.

I'd been offered a place of honor, at the center of the lives of those I'd adored the most. I'd watched over them in good times and bad, celebrated their triumphs and held them when they'd been too weak to stand.

Sure, I'd earned scuffs, rips, and leaks over the years, but I'd never trade any of them for a new life. I'd had the best role to play.

I'd seen it all and it wasn't over for me yet.

Looking out of the window at the grass gently blowing in the wind, I know there's a lot of life left in me. I'm ready to make more memories and take part in more adventures. I might get moved around from time to time, with long, lonely stretches in between, but I can be patient. I know my part now and I'll rejoice whenever I'm needed once again.

Because when you've been around as long as I have, you know you're so much more than a seat, or an accent chair—you're family.

ACKNOWLEDGMENTS

I doubt I'll ever properly express just how much this story means to me and what a joy it was to write it. I'd imagined writing a story about my beloved teal chair for years but struggled with the right way to approach it. It's difficult to explain how some stories come to be, but if I had to describe it, it would be something similar to a tiny seed being dropped into a wide cavity in the dirt. Covered up with more dirt, the concept begins to take root and germinate into a living, growing specimen, until it finally breaks through the ground into something we might manage to recognize as a story.

For me, the chair story had been one of those I'd been watering and cultivating for years, unsure of how to use it or its purpose until it all clicked into place. One day, it occurred to me that if the chair could speak, it would certainly have a whole lot to say about me and my family. After all, it had witnessed a whole lot.

This chair that had been a permanent figure in our everyday lives, photo bombing all our most cherished moments, with its fabric dangling and its leg oozing, over time, had carved a place inside my heart and made me wonder. What if this chair could talk, what would it say about our lives? If people can call boats, tractors, and cars by names, why not offer an entire persona to a chair?

So, for fun, I started imagining what the chair's perspective would be if it were given the opportunity to share it. In my mind, the chair's voice is that of Michael Caine's. To me, the refined seat deserved a dignified British accent. This set the tone for the story and the way the chair recounts it.

The love story between the chair and Queen Anne was a fun sideline that I would enjoy exploring some more later on, but for the purpose of this story, I decided to focus on the teal chair. There were so many elements to explore in this story. Subjects such as grief, loss, infertility, family, trust, hope, happiness, and so many more filled the pages, leaving me laughing or crying, depending on whatever passage I was working on.

This was most definitely a different project for me, but such a fun one. I enjoyed every minute I got to write about this chair, even when I was struggling to find the right way to end it. I had never intended for it to become a novella, but the chair's story kept growing past the appropriate length of a short story, so I just went with it. In true creative form, I ended up gaining inspiration for the last chapter by sitting in the teal chair to complete the story, deciding to write whatever I felt the chair wanted to say to the world.

A lot of what the chair has witnessed mirrors events that happened in my personal life, and I see this story as a precious testament of our lives during those years. Who knows, maybe this kind of book will become the new style of memoir? I doubt it, but it was such a wonderful experience to work on something so unique.

I still have the chair, of course. The bottom has been fixed up and rubber coasters have been placed beneath the leaky leg. It's my cat's favorite spot to nap and remains a sturdy and beautiful teal chair. I hope I get to enjoy it for many more years to come. We've been through a lot, me and this chair.

I'd like to say a special thank you to my parents for reading and cherishing this story alongside me. Another grateful thanks to my dad for fixing the bottom of the teal chair the year this was published, maybe in part because of the story. I'm sure the chair is grateful to feel decent again! I'd also like to express multiple gratitude to my dog, cat, and my eldest daughter for endless material to use in this story.

A big thanks to my writing critique groups for reading the first chapter and offering insights, while encouraging me to pursue this new line of thought and see it through. And to my husband for letting me go on and on about my ideas for where to take the story and listening to my excerpts, written frantically in the middle of the night, afraid it would escape my brain and miss the opportunity to actually make it in the book.

To my editor, Roxana Coumans, thank you for trying a new style with me, I'm so glad you enjoyed it as much as I did! Thanks to Arti, Jess, Karine, Mae, Willow, Renee, Gord, Rose, Chris, and all my readers on Instagram who eagerly awaited the chance to read this story in printed form. Thanks for not laughing at me when I mentioned writing a book from the perspective of a chair.

I hope this story makes you look at your cherished pieces of furniture and makes you think twice before discarding them. I hope it brings you joy to read this and provides lessons and enjoyment. This story might be short and sweet, but it is full of good nuggets that I hope will remain with you for a long time.

Enjoy!

Best Seat In The House

ABOUT THE AUTHOR

Michelle Young is a Canadian author of multiple books. She has been featured in The Globe and Mail, appeared on television and podcasts, and is passionately seeking new ways to bring invisible battles into the light through her stories. Young lives in the country on the outskirts of Ottawa with her family.

If you enjoyed this book, please make sure to leave a review and follow Michelle Young on Facebook, Instagram and Goodreads.
Facebook.com/michelleyoungauthor
Instagram @michelleyoungauthor
www.michelleyoungauthor

www.ingramcontent.com/pod-product-compliance
Lightning Source LLC
Chambersburg PA
CBHW021934170626
46807CB00007B/3099